Caught
in the Act

Caught
in the Act

Deb
Loughead

Orca currents

ORCA BOOK PUBLISHERS

Library and Archives Canada Cataloguing in Publication

Loughead, Deb, 1955-
Caught in the act / Deb Loughead.
(Orca Currents)

Issued also in electronic format.
ISBN 978-1-4598-0510-1 (bound).--ISBN 978-1-4598-0496-8 (pbk.)

I. Title.
PS8573.O8633C38 2013   jC813'.54   C2013-901921-9

First published in the United States, 2013
Library of Congress Control Number: 2013935384

Summary: Dylan is the suspect in robberies in a nearby cottage community.

MIX
Paper from
responsible sources
FSC® C016245
www.fsc.org

*Orca Book Publishers is dedicated to preserving the environment and has
printed this book on Forest Stewardship Council® certified paper.*

Orca Book Publishers gratefully acknowledges the support for its
publishing programs provided by the following agencies: the Government
of Canada through the Canada Book Fund and the Canada Council for the Arts,
and the Province of British Columbia through the BC Arts Council
and the Book Publishing Tax Credit.

Cover photography by Getty Images
Author photo by Steven Loughead

ORCA BOOK PUBLISHERS
PO Box 5626, Stn. B
Victoria, BC Canada
V8R 6S4

ORCA BOOK PUBLISHERS
PO Box 468
Custer, WA USA
98240-0468

www.orcabook.com
Printed and bound in Canada.

16 15 14 13 • 4 3 2 1

For Mike Orsini

Chapter One

"Dylan, you ready for this?" My friend Cory was breathless on the other end of the line. We'd been waiting for this day all month. It was the sweetest day of the entire summer, the first official day of summer vacation.

"I've been totally pumped for the past week, buddy! Ready and waiting."

"I'll meet you at the site. We're lighting it at three o'clock sharp," Cory told me.

"Sweet," I said. It was the same time school let out every day. "Start of another awesome summer! See ya over there, Cory."

I tried not to hear my mom's voice saying, *Dylan, maybe it's time for you to think about getting a job, to start paying for your own stuff and helping out around here a little bit.* I felt like sticking my fingers in my ears whenever she brought it up, but that would only make her mad. Jeez, I was still fifteen for a few more months. Couldn't a guy have at least one summer of freedom before being permanently chained to a job?

At that moment, the job thing wasn't a high priority. All I could think about was getting out and having some fun. And doing the Great Paper Blaze, a three-year tradition now. It was the perfect name for a schoolwork funeral pyre. I already had my backpack stuffed. I could hardly wait to watch it all go up in smoke.

I grabbed my backpack from my room and headed for the door. Only one escape route from our apartment, which meant I had to get past Gran without her asking me questions. That was never easy.

I had my hand on the doorknob. I turned it. I thought I was in the clear. Then I heard her clear her throat from where she was sitting on the sofa, watching her favorite program, The Weather Channel, and knitting socks as usual.

"Where you off to with that backpack, Dylan? I thought school was done already. Yesterday, wasn't it?"

I swear she can see in every direction at the same time. "Yep," I said, without looking at her. But I could practically feel her eyes burning into my skull. "Going to chill with Cory for a while." *Please don't remind me...*

"You told your mom you'd drop by and talk to the folks at Granitewood Lodge, remember? About working there this summer." She cleared her throat again in that knowing and annoying way.

I slipped out the door without answering. Then I ran all the way downstairs to grab my bike from the rack out back. In a few minutes I was cycling through streets that were already filling up with tourists and locals getting ready to party.

Here in Bridgewood, everyone goes a bit nuts on the first long weekend of summer. With school finally out and the start of summer-vacation season, it's definitely time to celebrate. And we invite everyone else to celebrate with us. Tourism is the bread and butter here, so we encourage it all summer long.

We lure people to town with special events like the farmers' market, arts and crafts shows and music festivals. The day-trippers show up in hordes. So do the city people, who arrive at their cottages for the long weekend and stick around all summer. *Cidiots*, my grandma likes to call them, because of their noisy personal watercraft. Those cottagers join the fun too. And Bridgewood is transformed from a ghost town into a holiday hub.

The town fills with seasonal workers this time of year, too, mostly college and university kids. They work at resorts for the summer to save money for school. The town population multiplies when the cottages, resorts and inns are packed with sun- and fun-loving vacationers looking for a getaway. Then the cash registers start to sing in all the shops and restaurants, including Rocky's Roadhouse, where my mom works as a bartender. Mom says the customers tip well, too, because they're mostly in a good mood.

As much as I resent the crowded streets sometimes, I can't blame the city folk for wanting to be here in Bridgewood. They couldn't pick a better place as far as awesome scenery goes. Our gleaming lake is the backdrop for the town, along with the granite outcroppings along the shore and our trademark gnarly pine trees stretching their limbs sideways. They make Bridgewood *the* place to be. In summer, anyway—winter is a whole other story.

I rode my bike out to the blaze site, which was a clearing in the woods. It wasn't too far from home. But nothing was in this town. All the other kids who were meeting us would have their backpacks filled with the past year's schoolwork too. The clearing was isolated enough that nobody could see what we were up to and make us stop.

"Hey, Dylan, what kept you?" someone called as I rode up.

"Yeah! We're ready to rock here," someone else said. It was barely three. Yet everyone was in a hurry for the annual ritual to begin.

Cory jogged over and gave me a high five. Then he pointed to the pit, which was set to be lit. It was already filled with crumpled and torn school notes, on top of a nice pile of dry kindling.

"Oh man, I am *so* ready for this," I said.

"Hey, here's Dillweed," someone said, and I cringed.

This was Garrett's favorite name for me. We hadn't been on good terms since a group of us got in deep doo-doo last winter for snowballing cars from a bridge and causing a car accident.

I knew he still held it against me that we had got nabbed. "Hey, Garrett," I said, flicking him a wave.

"So your granny let you come out and play today, huh?" he said. His friend Matt, who used to be my friend, thought that was pretty funny and laughed way too loud.

"Just ignore the losers," Cory said. "Hurry up and dump your backpack. It's time."

I dropped my bike, shrugged off my pack, unzipped it and dumped the contents onto the pile. Some of my friends clapped. My eyes searched the crowd for my friend Monica. But I knew I wouldn't see her. There were only a couple of girls in the crowd, and they'd come with their boyfriends.

Monica wasn't into stuff like this, and I couldn't blame her. *A lot of girls like to save school stuff forever*, Monica said when I invited her. *Including me.*

So not happening, Dylan. But when it came to being around Monica, I was ever hopeful. I still considered myself lucky that she'd forgiven me for being one of the jerks who caused her mom's car accident with those stupid snowballs.

"Who brought the matches?" Cory said. At least five kids reached into their pockets and pulled out a pack, and everyone grinned.

"Move in closer," Tanner said. This whole thing had been his idea a few years back, so he always got to call the shots. We all gathered around the fire pit.

"Okay, so this is it. The Great Paper Blaze and the start of summer vacation. Let's party on this summer! On three," Tanner said, then held up a can of lighter fluid and added a generous squirt to the fire. "One, two..."

"Three," we all yelled, and anyone who had a match lit and threw it.

WHOOSH! We all jumped back a few feet. The lighter fluid always did the trick. A sudden snapping and crackling, then licking and leaping orange flames, hot like the sun on our skin. Then smoke spiraled into the air and drifted up through the canopy of trees and into the crazy-blue sky. It was the official start of summer holidays.

We began to clap and cheer. A few of the guys let out earsplitting whistles through their fingers. Everyone was yelling and yammering at once. It was like a scene from *Lord of the Flies*. Some kids even started to do a wild fire dance. Others grabbed twigs and pinecones to toss in, because, after all, who can resist messing with a blaze? Especially one made with useless school notes.

Everyone shouted louder as the fire danced higher. Then it seemed to be getting a bit too high. Flaming tendrils whorled toward the maple branches that dangled over the clearing. I watched, my heart thudding hard, as leaves began to blacken and curl. Sure, the lake was close by, but we didn't even have a pail if this bonfire got out of control.

When I glanced at Cory, he looked as freaked as I was feeling. But nobody else seemed worried. They kept on yelling. It wasn't too tough to get caught up in the chaos. Everyone went into a frenzy, chanting, "School's out for the summer!"

That's probably why none of us heard the sirens.

Chapter Two

"What is going on here?" someone shouted. Then a dog barked. I recognized both voices and spun around. Officer Nicole Vance and her dog, Prince, were standing on the path at the edge of the clearing.

Uh-oh. Everyone froze, except for a few kids who hadn't heard her because they were hollering and whooping themselves. So she yelled again, even louder.

"Shut up, all of you!" That did the trick pretty fast. "The fire department is on the way."

I couldn't even look at Nicole. Maybe, if I was lucky, she hadn't noticed me.

"Oh, you're here, Dylan," she said. "Sorry to see that."

Nuts.

"Okay, everybody step away from the fire."

Nicole's face was taut and angry. She had one hand on her hip, the other hanging on to Prince's leash. Quite a few of the kids had done even better than step away. They'd taken off in all directions, like rats deserting a sinking ship.

"I know who you are," Nicole called as they bolted into the woods. "I probably went to school with your *parents*!"

Then she looked straight at me and sighed. "Dylan, whose bright idea *was* this stupid thing, anyway?"

I just looked at my shoes and shrugged.

By the time the firefighters had dragged a hose down the path from where the water-tank truck was parked and were starting to douse the blaze, Cory and I were the only ones left. Nicole stood shaking her head as clouds of smoke and steam rose skyward. The fire hissed and sputtered and finally died out.

"That could have had a way worse ending," a firefighter said, gazing at the soggy pit. "Whose dumb idea *was* it?" Then he looked at me.

I shrugged again. "Everybody's idea, I guess," I told him. "We've been doing it for a few years now."

"End-of-school ritual," Cory added. "Not such a great one, probably."

"Leave it to kids, huh?" Nicole said with a crooked grin. "Never know what they might pull on you next. Right, Dylan?"

Oh brother! Thanks for the reminder.

When I looked at Nicole, she was staring at me, and I felt my face start to burn. "Cory and I could have run away like everyone else did, you know," I said, trying to defend myself. "We weren't the *only* ones here, but we're getting the blame. *And* the lecture."

"I know that, Dylan. You're basically good kids," Nicole said. "Try and find some other way of celebrating, will you?"

"Don't worry, we will, Officer Vance," Cory said to Nicole. "Are you going to tell our parents?" There was panic in his eyes until she touched his shoulder in a soothing way.

"Well, I guess I can hang on to this one for now," she said. "And I *know*

Dylan will tell his mom and grandma before I do, won't you? Or should I mention to them how you missed that job interview you were supposed to have at three o'clock today?"

Why did Nicole and my mom have to be best friends? She knew everything about me!

"Headed there now," I told her. "Catch you later, Cory."

I grabbed my bike and took off along the trail. I was glad for an excuse to split, even if it meant sucking it up and trying to get a stupid summer job.

Granitewood Lodge wasn't one of those huge fancy chain resorts that everyone up here resented. It was a "charming and rustic bed-and-breakfast inn, tucked into the woods," according to my mom. Since opening the previous

May, it was already known for its nature walks and fine cuisine. It was attracting diners from all the cottages as well as from neighboring towns, Mom said. She and her new boyfriend, Brent, who drove up from the city most weekends, had loved the place both times they dined there.

The new owners had just finished renovating Granitewood when they stopped into Mom's bar for dinner one night. She'd told them I needed a job, of course, and they'd told her to send me over to talk to Mr. Hillier about it. Why did she have to get to know everyone in town? Mom figured I could be a busboy and maybe learn a thing or two about cooking so I could pitch in at home.

I leaned my bike on a hedge near the entrance and headed for the front door of the old timber lodge. It was one of those wooden screen doors that squeaked when you opened it. Inside, the lobby was cool and dim. A college-age girl stood behind the reception desk.

"Hi there," she said. "Are you and your parents checking in? Name, please."

I smiled at her. She was easy to smile at. "No, nothing like that," I said. "My name's Dylan O'Connor. I'm here for a job interview with Mr. Hillier. He said I should come by at—"

"Three o'clock," the girl said, staring at an ancient grandfather clock in a corner. "And it's three forty now, so you're forty minutes late. Mr. Hillier gave up waiting for you at three-oh-five. He doesn't think much of tardiness."

"Crap," I muttered under my breath. "I am *so* doomed."

"How come?" she asked, tilting her head in a pretty way. Her long dark hair hung like a veil to her shoulders. With those bangs, she reminded me of Zooey Deschanel.

"Long story, but basically my mom knows the Hilliers, and she tried to get a job for me. I got distracted on the way over here though. My friends were burning school notes out in the woods. And I didn't want to miss it—year-end ritual."

The girl nodded and smirked as she spun a pen on the countertop.

"Then we got caught when someone called nine-one-one and the cops and fire department showed up. So now, well, I'm doomed." *Wow. Way too much information. Why had I blabbed all that*? I shuffled toward the door and put my hand on the latch.

"Oh, I totally get it. Hang on, Dylan," she said. I turned around. "I'm Heather, *btw*. And you seem sweet. Let's see what I can do, okay?" Then she disappeared through a doorway leading to what appeared to be a dining room.

I looked around at all the antique tables and chairs in the lobby and the paintings of local scenery. I picked up a *Cottage Living* magazine from a table and leafed through it until I heard footsteps. When I looked up, Mr. Hillier was standing there. Behind him, Heather grinned, then winked.

"Oh, hi, Mr. Hillier," I said. I could feel myself starting to quake. "So sorry I'm late."

"No problem whatsoever, Dylan." He reached out and shook my hand. "I understand completely. It was nice of you to check up on that problem. So tell me, have you ever worked in a dining room or kitchen before?"

I glanced over his shoulder at Heather. She was nodding.

"Well, if cleaning up after supper counts, I have," I said and grinned. "And I can whip up a mean can of soup."

Mr. Hillier's eyes crinkled around the edges, and he started to laugh.

"Good one," he said. "Well, you seem like a responsible fellow. I think you'll make a fine busboy here. Consider yourself hired."

"Huh?" I said, blinking. "That's it?"

"Let's make it Tuesday morning, after the long weekend. So you can enjoy one last weekend of freedom. How does that sound?"

"Pretty great, I guess," I told him. "Wow. Thanks so much, sir." I shook his hand, and he winked at me.

"See you at eight sharp on Tuesday, Dylan." Then he spun around and walked away.

My mouth was hanging open, I was sure of it. When I looked at Heather, she had her hand slapped over her mouth, stifling her laughter.

"What just happened?" I said. "What was he talking about? *What* does he understand completely? *What* problem did I check up on?"

"That fire in the woods that those kids started. You saw the smoke when you were on your way over here, and you went to investigate. Then you called nine-one-one. Remember? That's why you were late for your interview." Heather was still grinning widely.

"Wait! You *told* him that?" Panic washed through me, and my legs turned all rubbery.

"Got you the job, didn't I? You should be *thanking* me, Dylan," she said. "Welcome to the staff at Granitewood Lodge. It's a great place to work."

"But the Hilliers know my mom! What if he says something to her? I'll be screwed." Now my mouth felt dry. Why did this dumb stuff keep happening to me today?

"Oh, don't stress out about it, Dylan. He won't even remember this happened.

He's always way too busy." She stepped forward and gave me a little hug. I didn't resist. She was soft and warm. Then the screen door creaked open, and a family burst inside.

"Welcome to Granitewood Lodge," Heather said, sidling back behind the desk. "How can I help you folks today?" She flicked me a quick finger wave and turned back to her customers.

Outside, I stood blinking in the bright sunshine. Somehow I'd managed to get myself a summer job. I was too confused to figure out if I was happy about it or not.

"Good for you, Dylan!" Mom beamed at me from behind the bar at Rocky's Roadhouse when I went in to break the "good" news. "I figured you'd get the job. You're such a mature and responsible guy these days."

That nearly made me choke on a sip of Coke. I swirled the ice cubes with my straw.

"Um, there's something you should know before you get too excited, Mom," I said, and her smile melted. She spun around like she was afraid to hear what I needed to tell her. She grabbed a plate of nachos from the kitchen ledge and set it on the counter in front of a man who was reading. Then she leaned on the counter and sighed.

"What happened this time, Dylan?"

"Okay, so it's not that bad, you know, and I wasn't the only one there." Then I told her about the fire, and she listened calmly as she made slow circles on the bar with a damp towel. Not even looking at me. When I finished, I waited. And, whew, she actually smiled again.

"At least you stuck around instead of bolting. And you're right, Nicole would have told me for sure." When she patted my hand, I felt myself relax a bit. "That could have turned out awful though. Use your head, Dylan, okay? Promise you'll stay smart this summer."

The man at the bar was smiling as he eavesdropped. "Bigger the kid, bigger the problem," he said. "Trust me, it doesn't get any easier, Stephanie."

"Gee, thanks, John," Mom said, forcing a smile. "That's the last thing I needed to hear."

Chapter Three

Friday evening I had only three more days of freedom. Yet there I was, stuck at home with Gran, with zip all to do. Cory had some family birthday party happening. The evening seemed to stretch ahead like a colossal yawn. I sat in front of a screen in my room, steering a speeding car with my controller and wishing something cool would happen.

Then, like magic, the phone rang, and I grabbed the portable in my room.

"So did you get the job?" It was Cory. I had to use a landline because Mom wouldn't let me have a cell phone in such a small town. It was pointless, she said, and she was probably right.

"Yeah, got it," I said, but I didn't explain exactly *how* I got it. I'd be holding on to that.

"Cool. I *guess*." He sounded almost disappointed. "So why don't you come over and stay here tonight? My folks and sister are going out now to celebrate some more with the family, and I don't feel like going with them. Mom said you could come over, since they'll be home late."

"Be there in fifteen," I said, then hung up and headed for the door.

I still had to get past Gran. She was playing Solitaire on the coffee table in front of a *Frasier* rerun.

"Going to Cory's. Sleeping there. See ya tomorrow, Gran." My hand was on the knob.

"Hold it," she said, then turned around to look at me. "Does your mom know? Did you even call to tell her?"

"I will when I get there," I said, then opened the door a crack.

"Where's your overnight stuff, Dylan? You know, pajamas, toothbrush, change of clothes. Etcetera."

"Gran, I sleep in my boxers in the summer. I keep a toothbrush at Cory's. It's all good."

"Don't forget to call your mom," she said, but her voice was muffled by the door that I'd closed behind me.

"Right, Gran," I called back to her.

Then I ran all the way down six flights of stairs and grabbed my bike from the bike rack.

The heat was stifling, and it was so humid, it was like riding through smothering steam. My clothes stuck to me instantly, and within a few minutes I could feel the sweat trickling down my back. With this hot weather so early, it was shaping up to be the perfect summer. Too bad I had to miss it being stuck with a job.

Cory was waiting on his porch when I wheeled into his driveway. He came down the steps and slapped my hand.

"Come on inside," he said. "Got a new video game to show you."

Great. I'd just left a boring screen, and now I had to sit in front of another one. But it was his house, so he got first shot on the plans. Which is why, an hour later, we were still sitting in front of a screen shooting at stuff in some sort of new military game. His house was hot, and I was sweltering. He said the AC wasn't working properly, and that wasn't working well for me. I half wished I had an excuse to leave, but I couldn't come up with one. Till the phone rang.

Cory answered, and his face dropped. "It's your gran," he said. "She sounds mad."

"Oops. I knew I forgot something. I'll try and calm her down." I grabbed the receiver.

But I couldn't get a word in edgewise. She was furious. Mom had called home to talk to me, and Gran told her I was at Cory's place and was supposed to have called the bar to let her know when I arrived. So Mom was worried that something had happened to me on the way over. Which explained the frantic call from Gran. And the order from Mom to come home for the night instead of sleeping over. *Nuts*!

"Okay, okay, Gran," I said, trying to soothe her. "I totally forgot. I'm sorry! I'll be there in a little while. Yep, before eleven. I promise." I hung up and looked at Cory. "I wish they wouldn't freak out so much over me. Let's at least go for a bike ride before I have to get home. I'm sick of being inside."

That's how we wound up running into Tanner a few minutes later.

"Hey, guys!" Tanner waved at us from under a streetlight, where he stood with another guy. I recognized him. Tanner's cousin Jacob, who always visited for summer vacations. We rode over to them. I still had nearly an hour before I had to be home.

"What's up?" I said.

"Well, we were thinking—" Jacob was grinning as he looked at Tanner.

"That since it's so stinking hot tonight—" Tanner grinned back.

"We should head over to the secret beach for a skinny dip," Jacob said. "I mean, look at those stars!" He swept his hand across the inky sky, which was thick with stars and a crescent moon.

"Sure don't get that in the big city. Be even better at the beach."

"Okay, I'm in," I said. "Since my freedom's running out. Starting a job at Granitewood Lodge on Tuesday."

"That sucks," Tanner said.

"I know," I said. "But Mom wants me to start helping out at home. Anyway, it'll be cool to be able to buy my own stuff without begging, for a change. So you up for this, Cory?"

Cory's face was twisted, as if he was having a debate in his head.

"I'm not sure," he said. "I was supposed to stay home. This is already stretching it."

"But it's the first day of vacation," said Tanner. "And that whole note-burning thing this afternoon turned out so lame."

"Oh, *whatev*," said Cory. "Let's do this, dudes!"

Cory and I dropped our bikes at the top of the hill. A set of log steps had been built into the steep bank leading down to the beach. Pale moonlight seeped through the trees and shivered out across the water. We scrambled down behind Tanner and Jacob, half on our butts because the old steps were half buried in undergrowth. At the bottom, we stood on a gleaming crescent of sand and let the lapping waves lick our toes.

"Wow, it's so warm," Jacob said, then started to whip off his clothes.

In a few seconds we were all wading into the warm shallows, then diving under like a bunch of nocturnal otters to swim farther out.

I was the first one to spot the flash-light beam bobbing around in the trees onshore. It was farther along, beyond where the beach ended, above a craggy hunk of granite where I knew there was a path. Kids liked to sit on the rocks there and fish, since there was a deep pool at the bottom. On nights like this, though, they liked to sit on the rocks and do other stuff.

"Quiet for a sec," I said. "We don't want them to notice us. So don't move."

We swam closer to shore, where the moonlight wouldn't give us away. Then we stood in water up to our chests, watching. The guys on the rock were being stealthy themselves, talking in low whispers with the odd rumbly laugh. I had the feeling they might be "getting up to no good," as Gran would say. And warned me *not* to be doing. Ever.

The clock was ticking toward eleven and my curfew. But I was stuck in the lake with my friends. Our clothes were on the shore. If we made a move, the guys on the rock would spot us for sure. And they had a flashlight.

"What should we do now?" Cory murmured beside me. "I'm starting to get cold. If we head for shore, they might see us."

"So *what* if they see us?" Tanner said, not even trying to whisper. "Who cares?"

"Be *quiet*, Tanner," I told him. "Let's wait a few minutes. Maybe they'll leave."

There were plenty of jerks in this town. I didn't want to run into any of them in my current state of nakedness.

"I'm going back anyway. I want to get out of here. *Like right now*." Cory started to wade in. It almost looked as if he was tiptoeing through the water to avoid being spotted from shore.

"Quit being such a suck, Cory," Tanner said. "They're not gonna bother us." Then he dove and started to swim, splashing up a noisy storm with his arms.

The flashlight flicked our way, and the bright LED beam poured over the dark water. "Someone's out there," somebody said. It was a voice I knew. That was a bad thing. "Let's go check it out," another guy said. Another familiar voice.

Then the light began to bounce across the rocks and along the path toward the secret beach. Some secret.

"Crap," I said. "Nice work, Tanner."

Chapter Four

Tanner had stopped swimming. We all waded over to him and waited. The thin slice of moon felt like a searchlight shining down on us. We kept low in the water. I watched the flashlight as it closed in on the beach, and I held my breath. Then the beam landed on our clothes.

"Dudes!" one of them called. The light danced across the water. "You guys swimming nekked out there or what?"

Judging from the dead silence, none of us had the guts to answer. By that point, we all knew exactly who was standing on the shore with a flashlight. Garrett and his nasty band of followers.

"Come on, don't be shy, guys." Low chuckles, but not from any of us.

"Probably don't want to attract any attention," one of them said. "Watch this."

In the circle of light on the beach, I saw something fly through the air, and my heart sank.

"What are they *doing*?" Jacob said.

"Pitching our clothes up in the trees," I said. "Double *crap*."

Tick, tick, tick. I was getting more doomed every second. The guys on the beach were killing themselves laughing as they tossed our clothes as high as they could into the tree branches. In the beam of their light I could see boxers, shorts and T-shirts, including my favorite one, flapping up there like laundry hung out to dry.

After that, the guys taunted us for a bit, their voices oozing smugness. Then they got bored, I figured. Because we never budged, even though we were all shivering now. I held my breath as I watched them wander away. Their bouncing ray of light grew dim and finally disappeared into the woods. Then we waded back to shore.

We stood there in the sand, looking up at the ghostly shapes of our clothes dangling from the branches of the pine trees overhead. There was not a chance we could reach them. We tried throwing rocks to knock them down, but that didn't work. We found a long dead branch in the woods and tried to reach them with that, but still no dice.

"Well, boys," I finally said. "Anybody got a Plan B? I mean, unless you're okay with walking through town like this. I don't think anyone else would be okay with it."

Tanner and Jacob dropped a few choice swear words as they blew off steam about what Garrett and his buddies had done to us. Cory's face was screwed up like he was either thinking hard or about to cry. I wasn't sure which. If only we had towels, at least.

Then I got an idea. "Wait," I said.

"Wait *what*, Dylan?" Tanner said. "Any idea will be a good one right now, trust me."

"How about if we check out some of the cottages nearby and see if anyone has towels hanging around?" I said.

"Hmm, guess we could 'borrow' them. Then return them tomorrow when we come back with a pole or some-thing to get our clothes out of the trees,"

Cory said. "That's actually not a bad idea, dude."

"Okay, so let's do this," I said.

I ignored the alarm bells that were clanging in my head. We had no other choice. We had to try this, even though the thought of it made me wince. If only Gran and Mom could see me now. Oh, and of course Mr. Hillier. His "responsible" new employee. They'd all be so proud!

We stumbled along the shore path, traipsing across cottage property lines in our desperate towel hunt. Whenever security lights flicked on, we ducked behind bushes and kept to the shadows. We passed plenty of boathouses and deck chairs, but no towels.

"So where're all the towels?" Tanner said. "I mean, everyone swims from their docks."

"Probably hanging from clothes-lines closer to their cottages," Cory said. "We'll have to check there, maybe."

"We're screwed if someone spots us," Jacob said.

"Got to risk it, guys, if we ever want to get home tonight," I said, and then I pushed my way through the undergrowth, heading for the yellow light that spilled through the window of the nearest cottage. As we edged through the trees and closed in on the deck, I spotted it. A row of beach towels hanging from the deck rail. I turned to my friends and waved them on.

But a sudden flash stopped us in our tracks before we got there. Then there was another flash. And another and another, with every move we made.

"Crap!" I said. "Freeze, guys. It's a motion sensor."

Cory dropped to the ground, and the rest of us followed his lead. Then, hunkered close to the ground, we crab-walked toward the deck. And each snatched a towel. A dog started to bark, deep and loud, like he meant business. We wrapped our towels around us and took off around the corner of the cottage, heading for the road like we were being chased by banshees. Tanner and Jacob went in one direction. Cory and I headed for the bikes we'd left at the top of the hill. Then we rode off in opposite directions without even saying goodbye.

Thank goodness the apartment door was unlocked. I slipped inside slowly and shut the door with a soft click. Gran always waited up till Mom got home from work, but most of the time she dozed off. And this time, whew, I could see she was asleep on the sofa, slumped sideways, with her legs curled up. I could see the time on the DVD player. It was well past 11:30. I dashed for the hallway and my bedroom.

"Dylan?" Gran's sleepy voice. "That you? What time is it?"

"Got home awhile ago," I said. "Just going to the washroom. You totally slept through it, Gran."

Must have worked. She didn't say another word. And I dove between my sheets, leaving the filched towel on the floor beside my bed. So glad that today was finally over. Because there was no way that tomorrow could possibly ever be as bad as today had been.

The next morning, when I sat on the side of my bed to get dressed, it only took me a few seconds to realize that the towel was gone. *Uh-oh.* My gut instantly began to churn. I could hear voices in the living room. I checked my clock. It was past nine.

I opened my bedroom door and edged along the hallway. Mom, Gran and Officer Nicole were sitting there. The stolen beach towel was on the coffee table. Mom, with her radar hearing, spun her head as if I'd just said something.

"Oh, good morning, Dylan," she said. "Any idea where this towel came from?"

"Um, what towel, Mom?" *Nice one, Dylan.*

"I wonder who was getting up to no good last night?" Gran said, eyeing me.

"Mom, I told you *not* to say that," my mom told Gran. "Really, I think he knows he's in a whack of trouble by now, don't you?"

"Trouble?" My mouth was dry, as if I'd been eating soda crackers. "For what?"

Then I realized Nicole was holding a camera.

"Come over here and I'll show you," she said, patting the sofa beside her.

I sure didn't want to go there, but I had no choice.

Chapter Five

Turned out it wasn't a motion-sensor light after all. It was a motion-sensor *camera*! With an SD memory card. Which Nicole now had in her own camera.

The camera had been hanging in a tree. The nature-crazy cottagers liked to photograph the animal night-life. They had photos of wolves, bears and deer that had crossed their property in the dark. And photos of US! Luckily, you couldn't see much in the four shots. But my shocked face was definitely caught in the flash before we hit the ground and scrambled away. *Only* mine in the spotlight. The other three guys all had their heads turned. *Crap*! *Why me*?

"Not a big deal," I said, trying to sound as if I believed myself. "Because we're returning the towels today. When we go back for our clothes." My face was burning big-time because of the looks on all their faces. "As you can tell by the photos, we were in a bit of a jam. We couldn't exactly knock on the door and ask to borrow them."

"Yes, I get that." Mom cringed. "But you know there's never a good excuse for stealing. So what happened to your clothes?"

"Borrowed," I said. "We *borrowed* those towels. We had no choice. Some jerks at the beach threw our clothes up in the trees. And we needed to get home without mooning the town. They're still hanging there, if you want proof."

"*What* jerks at the beach?" the three ladies said at once.

"Just some goofballs *up to no good.*" I glared at Gran. True. And there was no way I planned on ratting out Garrett. He was one guy I didn't want mad at me. "And Tanner and his cousin Jacob were there swimming too. *Not* just me and Cory."

Silence. The three of them stared at me. Then Mom sighed.

"Okay, so it's not so much about the swimming or the towels," Mom said. "And it's not even about you breaking house rules either. As lousy as all that is. Tell him the rest, Nicole."

"Last night a cottage near these folks got broken into, Dylan," Nicole explained, tapping her camera. "When these people heard the news this morning, they recalled how their dog had barked last night. So they checked their motion-sensor camera. That was when they realized their towels were gone. And when they found your photos on the camera, they handed the memory card over to us."

I gulped. "So what does *that* mean?" I said.

Nicole squinted at me. "It means that you and your friends are suspects, Dylan. Since you were nearby around the time of the break-in. And you actually stole something last night."

"*Borrowed*!"

"Tell me what you know, Dylan," Nicole said. "It could help save your hide."

"From what?" Now I was getting angry. I was in trouble for doing practically nothing wrong, yet they didn't seem to believe me. "What got stolen from that cottage, anyway?"

"Can't tell you," Nicole said. "Might compromise the investigation. The owners were having dinner at Granitewood Lodge. They don't have an alarm. The thieves climbed through an open window."

"Well, those cottager *cidiots* are pretty dumb then, aren't they?" I said. Right away, I regretted saying that. "I don't *know* who it was, Nicole. Trust me, it was major dark down at the beach. We never even saw their faces." At least that was true. I hated withholding information from Nicole.

"*And*," Nicole added solemnly, "this isn't the first break-in around here lately either."

They were all staring at me. "I don't *know* anything. What are you all staring at?"

"Don't be bold," Gran said. Then she picked up her knitting, and her fingers started to fly as the needles clicked like mad. That usually meant she was upset. I had a feeling they all were.

"I'm not sure I like where this is going," Mom told me. "The summer has just started, and look what's happened already. Thank goodness you got a job. That'll keep you out of trouble."

I offered her a weak smile, then looked at Nicole. "So are we charged with something or what?" I said.

"Don't know yet. Depends on what happens next. Now go brush your teeth. We're going for a car ride to check out those clothes hanging from the trees." Her smile seemed to say this would be an adventure, but I had my doubts.

"But it's close by," I reminded her. "We could walk, you know."

"When have you ever passed up a ride in my cruiser?" Nicole said with a wink. "Besides, there's some other stuff to get done too."

I didn't like where *this* was going. Mom's and Gran's mouths looked like Venus flytraps. "But I haven't even had breakfast yet," I said, still stalling.

"Isn't that what Timmy's is for?" Nicole said as she headed for the door.

Officer Nicole stood on the beach, sipping her coffee and staring up at the trees. The chunk of bear claw I'd been chewing on stuck in my throat as I followed her gaze.

"So where are they, Dylan?" she said, shaking her head.

I looked in every direction. Even out on the water. Had last night been a dream or what? Where the heck had all our clothes gone?

"I mean, seriously. I want to believe you, but your story keeps getting shakier. What's going on here? " She sipped her coffee again, then took a bite of bagel.

"Honestly, I have no clue," I said with a shrug. "Maybe they blew away?"

"Wrong answer, bud," Nicole said.

"Sorry, but it's the best one I've got," I said, not even hiding my sarcasm.

Nicole frowned at me. "Let's go pick up your friends," she said. "Maybe they can help us figure out this mystery."

My stomach plummeted. Cory's folks would not be thrilled about this. Neither would Tanner's and Jacob's. But why should I have to take all the heat, I told myself as Nicole steered her cruiser toward Cory's place. Besides, maybe one of them would rat out Garrett and his friends so I wouldn't have to. At least Prince wasn't in the back-seat, panting on my neck and making me more nervous.

As far as nastiness went, today had yesterday beat already, and it wasn't even noon yet.

Chapter Six

The other guys' parents insisted on taking them to the station to give their statements. I was stuck alone in the cruiser with Nicole. I slumped down so nobody would notice me.

She explained as she drove that we each had to tell our stories separately, so the police could see if they matched. At the station, the four of us sat on a bench outside the interrogation room and waited to be called in. We were practically vibrating, we were so scared. But none of us said a word. The other guys' parents stood in a corner, whispering. They shot worried glances at us every now and then.

I let everyone else go ahead of me so that they'd all be gone by the time I got out. I sure didn't want to face the wrath of their parents. I figured I wouldn't be seeing much of the guys for a while after this. And I knew Nicole would have to tell their folks about the paper fire yesterday, too. My friends would probably be grounded for the summer. And I wouldn't be very popular for telling Nicole they'd been there.

Turned out it wasn't Nicole who interviewed us. It was another cop, Officer Donahue. He looked sort of scary, with a thick neck and a head to match. No wonder the guys had looked so freaked out when they left that interrogation room. When he came to the door and motioned for me to come in, I felt like exiting stage left. That might have looked bad though.

"Sit down, Dylan," he said. I sat down across from him. The room was empty except for the table and two chairs, like in movies. There was a tape recorder on the table. He had a notepad in front of him. It all made me feel like a criminal.

The officer cleared his throat. "So tell me what you were up to last night, buddy. Take your time. Make sure you get your story straight. And we'll take it from there, okay?"

He didn't sound as mean as he looked. He sort of smiled. I took a deep breath and started to talk. Officer Donahue took notes the whole time. He looked up at me every now and then. I'm pretty sure he was mostly grinning when I got to the skinny-dip part. He didn't even ask any questions either. Just took my statement.

I took a chance and never mentioned Garrett's name, because it was dark, and what if I was wrong? What if it wasn't him after all, and I got him in trouble for nothing? In a few minutes it was all over. Officer Donahue stood up and patted my shoulder and told me I could leave.

I slipped out the door of the station without even looking for Nicole to say goodbye. The hot July sun felt fantastic on my face after being in that stuffy room. On the main drag, the sidewalks were crowded with tourists. I set off across town for home, glad for the time to be alone to think.

Something weird had happened around the time our clothes were thrown into the trees and we'd left the woods, wrapped in those swiped towels. A cottage had been robbed. And this morning all our clothes were missing. What was going on? It was as if Garrett and his friends had tried to cover up their tracks. That way, we'd have to take the blame. It was starting to look like a setup. How could I prove it though? And would Garrett actually commit a robbery?

A finger of guilt began to prod me. I thought maybe I should go back and confess to Nicole what I knew about last night. At least it might be a lead in her investigation. It sure would be a huge weight off my mind if I told her. I was about to turn back when something stopped me.

Through the crowd ahead of me, I caught sight of a pretty face and dark silky hair. It was Heather, from the lodge, heading my way. She spotted me and smiled. She was holding hands with a guy I didn't recognize.

When I saw what he was wearing, I froze in the middle of the sidewalk. A lady bumped into me, then jostled on past.

I still couldn't move. Because I couldn't tear my eyes off the gray T-shirt the guy was wearing. It was totally unique, with a cool skateboarding skeleton design, made by an indie skate company on the east coast. I didn't know anyone who had a T-shirt like that.

Except for me—until last night.

The guy in my T-shirt veered into a bakery, and Heather headed straight for me. She wrapped me in another one of those soft hugs. I half wished she wouldn't let go.

"Hey, Dylan! How *are* you!" I swear her smile could make birds fall out of the sky.

"Hi, Heather." I tried not to look too sappy when she let go of me. "Not working today?"

"Yep, I am, actually. Noon-till-eight shift. Just hanging out with Hayden for a bit before we have to head over to the lodge."

"Oh, so he works there too," I said, getting more curious.

"Of course, dum-dum. He's Hayden *Hillier*. The *boss's* son. He actually *lives* there. He's picking up some supplies for his dad."

Gulp. As she said that, Hayden walked out of the store with a huge bag of fresh buns.

"How's it going?" he said. "Want a bun? They're still warm." Heather helped herself.

Trying not to stare too hard at my favorite T-shirt, I shook my head.

"Nice shirt," I said. I couldn't resist. "Where'd you get it, anyway?"

"Awesome, huh? It was a...a gift." *Yeah right!*

"Hayden, this is Dylan O'Connor," Heather said. "He's starting at the lodge on Tuesday."

"That's cool," Hayden said, then walked over to check out a music-shop window.

"Man of few words," she said, laughing. "So I guess I'll see you Tuesday."

Then she did it again. Reached out and wrapped me in another soft, cozy hug. I didn't resist. After all, when would I ever have another chance to be hugged by a college girl? Over her shoulder, I spotted someone else in the crowd. My friend Monica Buckley, her face questioning. When our eyes met, she spun around and walked fast in the opposite direction. I let go of Heather and took off after her.

"Monica, wait," I called, but she didn't stop until my hand was on her shoulder.

"*What*, Dylan?" she said. When she turned to look at me, I saw hurt in her eyes. And I felt a thrill inside. This girl honestly cared about me. "And who was *she*, anyway?"

"Heather. She works at the lodge. Where my *job* starts Tuesday," I told her, grinning.

This time she smiled too. "You got the job? Cool. So do you know her, or what?"

"I met her there yesterday," I said. "She works on the reception desk. She's one of those real huggers. She was with her boyfriend, Hayden Hillier, just now."

Monica seemed to relax when I told her that. "The boss's son. Wow. Lucky her. I hear they're loaded. Hey, so guess what happened last weekend?"

"I'm sure you'll tell me," I said. We walked along, shoulders touching and fingers laced together. It was easy to forget Heather's hugs while Monica was holding my hand.

"Somebody tried to break into my mom's friend's cottage. She called to tell my mom about it today." She was breathless, as if the thought of it scared her.

I stopped and stared at her. "Did it happen last night?" I said. "While they were having dinner at Granitewood Lodge?"

Monica frowned. "No, it was last weekend. Their alarm went off and scared the thieves away. But how did you know they were eating at Granitewood Lodge that night?"

"You mean *they* were eating there too?" I said, and Monica yelped.

"Ouch! You squeezed my hand too hard." She yanked it free. "You're the one who said they were eating there, Dylan."

I stood on the sidewalk, blinking and thinking. Monica stared at me. Strolling shoppers grumbled when they had to swerve around the two of us. *Two* of the robbery victims had been eating there on separate nights? "*Something is rotten in the state of Denmark*," I murmured.

"You're quoting *Hamlet*? Seriously?" Monica said. She nudged me with her shoulder. "How come you're standing there in a daze, Dylan?"

"Because I think I figured something out. And I almost wish I hadn't," I said.

As we headed toward her house, I told Monica the rest of the story. She smiled knowingly when she found out how the fire department had shown up out in the woods yesterday. And she couldn't help but laugh when she heard about our clothes dangling in the trees. And the camera in the woods. When she heard the rest, though, she was instantly curious.

"You mean Hayden Hillier was wearing your T-shirt? That's bizarre!"

"Exactly. What does that mean? The clothes are missing from the trees, and now he has my T-shirt. Was he there last night, throwing our clothes up in the trees with Garrett and the other guys? Did they go and rob that cottage? Then take our clothes later to cover up their tracks? See where I'm going with this? The boss's son at Granitewood Lodge—"

"Could be a *thief*?" Monica grabbed my arm. "You think he *did* it, Dylan? Along with Garrett?"

"It's starting to look that way," I said. "I just need more proof. When I start work on Tuesday, I'm looking for it. Pretty strange that robberies happened when the cottage owners were eating dinner at Granitewood."

We stopped in front of the ice-cream parlor. They made the ice cream right in the store. My favorite was Chocolate Monkey, rich dark chocolate with peanut-butter chunks. Yum. I wanted to treat Monica to her favorite, Banana Orange Tango. When we stepped outside with our cones, a cruiser glided up to the curb. It was Nicole, and this time she had Prince in the backseat, panting over her shoulder. He was an amazing dog, but I'd never want to be on the receiving end of those teeth during a takedown.

"Dylan, I'm heartbroken! You never said goodbye after our date this morning." She grinned at me through the window.

"Hah. Hilarious, Nicole," I said, shaking my head in disgust.

"Hi, Monica." Nicole gave her a wave. "So, good news, Dylan. All your stories matched up. You and your friends are off the hook. And I'm back at square one."

I forced a smile. Clearly, the others hadn't ratted out Garrett. Now it was all on my head.

"I guess I am too, Nicole," I told her. "But I'll let you know if I come up with anything."

"Hope so," she said, and then the cruiser drove off slowly along the busy street.

"You didn't tell her everything you know," Monica said. "Why not, Dylan?"

I thought about that as I took a lick of Chocolate Monkey. "I'm starting a new job on Tuesday. And it might not be a great idea to rat out the boss's son before that. Especially when I don't know enough yet. I mean, what if that T-shirt *was* a gift, and I got it all wrong?"

"Good way to lose a job—which you didn't want in the first place though," Monica said with a sly grin. She'd made a good point. But now I kind of wanted the job after all. Plus, I had a whole lot of snooping to do at the lodge.

"I'll see what happens next week, Monica. But now I just want to enjoy the rest of the long weekend. And I hope you feel like doing the same thing."

By the way Monica smiled at me, I knew her answer was yes.

Chapter Seven

The rest of the weekend was pretty much perfect. On Sunday morning, Mom's boyfriend Brent rented a boat and took me, Mom, Gran and Monica for a long cruise out on the lake. Mom was practically delirious to have a whole day off in the middle of a long weekend. She never stopped smiling. We ate lunch on a restaurant patio overlooking the bay, and Brent treated us all.

None of my friends called, but Cory messaged me on FB to say he was grounded for the weekend and hoped I'd find something to do without his help. No problem. Monica was sitting beside me at the computer when I read it, and she hugged me and laughed.

I had dinner at her place on Sunday evening, since Mom was busy with Brent. Then we spent the holiday Monday hanging out at the community docks, fishing and swimming. The highlight, though, was watching the evening fireworks with Monica from a log at the secret beach. The night blazed with explosions of color that lit the sky and reflected across the bay. But the best part was when Monica leaned in and kissed me.

After that, I *so* didn't want the weekend to end and Tuesday to come, but there was no stopping it.

I woke up late on Tuesday morning. I couldn't believe it. I thought I'd set my alarm clock for six thirty so I'd have plenty of time. But I'd accidentally set it for seven thirty. I only had half an hour to shower, grab breakfast and then pedal my bike across town to Granitewood Lodge.

Which is why I was riding like mad at seven fifty, chewing on a granola bar and trying to make up for lost time. So it wasn't great when I spotted the cruiser coming toward me. And even worse when it stopped at the corner and Nicole waved me over.

"Good news, Dylan," she said. "One of your friends 'fessed up. He told us who threw the clothes into the trees on Friday night. So now I have my robbery suspects." Then she frowned. "Why didn't you tell me yourself, anyway?"

I could hardly believe what she was saying. Or maybe I could. Maybe one of my friends was desperate to get back some summer freedom. Maybe he had to rat out Garrett in order to save his own skin.

"So who was it?" I said, still wondering if this was a trick to pry the truth out of me.

"Why don't you tell me?" Nicole said, then smiled.

"Because I don't want to accuse the wrong person," I said. Which was the total truth.

Nicole squinted in her perceptive way. "You know more, don't you, Dylan?" she said.

"The only thing I know for sure is that I'm almost late for my first day of work," I said. Then I steered my bike past her cruiser and on toward the lodge.

I parked my bike in a rack around back but went in through the front door again. And I was half disappointed that Heather wasn't there, waiting to give me a hug. In fact, nobody was there. I could hear voices and the clatter of dishes and cutlery coming from the kitchen. I figured I'd probably be hearing that sound a lot this summer.

"Hello?" I called. "Anybody home?"

"Dylan! Good morning." Mr. Hillier appeared in the dining room doorway. "Right on time. I like that in an employee. Let me show you around. We'll start here."

In the first hour, I learned a whole lot about how things worked at the lodge. Nobody was officially on the reception desk until noon, when Heather started her shift. That was also when the dining room opened for lunch. Until then, if we heard the desk bell ding, one of us from the kitchen was to come out and see who was there. Kitchen staff were also to answer the phone and take dinner reservations that came in during the morning.

That first morning on the job, I learned about clearing the tables after the lodge guests had finished their buffet breakfasts. The biggest surprise was how much food people wasted. I was so tempted to scarf down a Danish left behind on a plate. But that would look bad if I got caught, so I scraped it into the garbage along with everything else and loaded the dishes into the dishwasher. Half-empty yogurt cups, half-eaten omelets and slices of toast…Gran would have been mortified.

I took a few phone calls as well, since Tony, the line chef, and Kelly, a server, were busy with food prep. I used my most polite voice for those calls. In the reservation book, I took down the names and phone numbers of people booking tables. I even asked them to repeat their information to avoid mistakes.

I kept my eyes and ears wide open, wondering if I could pick up any clues to help Nicole. But it seemed pointless. If there was any connection between the robberies and the fact that both victims were eating here when they happened, I sure couldn't find it.

Hayden Hillier showed up around ten and got busy in the kitchen. Today he *wasn't* wearing my T-shirt. I saw him checking out menus and talking to the chef. I got the feeling that he was training to become a chef himself. He took a couple of phone calls at the desk after he got there, too. Heather showed up just before noon. She came over and gave me a hug again. I wished it didn't feel so good. Then I wished I hadn't had to wish that.

Lunch hour was busy, and I didn't even look at the clock. After the paying customers were taken care of, Hayden handed me a thick ham-and-cheese sandwich. This job had its good points. Before I knew it, Mr. Hillier popped into the dining room, where I was finishing setting tables for the dinner hour.

"Dylan, we don't encourage over-time work here," he said, grinning.

I checked the wall clock. It was four fifteen. "Wow, today zoomed by," I told him.

"Nice job, buddy. See you tomorrow," Mr. Hillier said, then patted my back as I went past him to hang up my apron.

I could hardly believe that my first day on the job was already over. Even though I would never admit it to Mom and Gran, I was actually looking forward to day two. I pedaled home along the main drag on yet another bright and steamy afternoon. At the variety shop, I hit the brakes, dropped my bike and ran in for a Freezie. While I was waiting to pay, Garrett's mom showed up. When she spotted me, her face dropped. *Nuts.*

"Oh, it's *you*, Dylan. Garrett's out in the car. He's in deep trouble. It was just a silly *prank*, you know." She glared at me, then headed for the counter. I dashed for the door.

There was no avoiding Garrett though. His mom's car was parked in a space right in front of the store. He was in the passenger seat, looking totally miserable. When he saw me, his face hardened.

"We were just goofing around on Friday night, Dylan. Why did you rat us out, anyway?"

"It wasn't me." I kept my distance from the car. "It was probably one of the *other* guys you messed with that night."

For the first time ever, Garrett looked like he was about to cry. "You gotta help me. Now we're robbery suspects. We're screwed. And you can get us off the hook."

"But the robbery happened the same night you were wandering around with flashlights," I reminded him. "How can we even be sure it wasn't you? And what happened to our clothes?"

"We went back with a golf-ball retriever to knock the clothes down after you left. We were trying to hide the evidence in case you guys ratted us out. One of the guys threw them in some garbage bin." Now he actually looked as if he was sorry about the whole thing.

"Blew up in your face, didn't it?" I said, feeling smug for once. "You'd look like less of a thief if you told Nicole what bin our clothes got tossed in."

"We did, but they weren't there when she went to check," Garrett said.

"Hah. That happened to us too. When *we* were suspects and I had to show Nicole our clothes in the trees for proof. And they weren't there. We got in trouble because of *you*. I guess that's why one of my friends ratted you out. To get *us* off the hook."

"So who's gonna save *our* hides now?" he said, looking even more distressed.

Hmm…I had a feeling I knew where those clothes might have wound up.

"Leave it with me, Garrett," I said.

"*Seriously*? You *know* something, Dylan?" Wow, he hadn't even called me Dillweed yet. I was starting to like this situation.

"If I get this figured out, then you owe me big-time, okay?" I said.

Garrett held his hand out the window for a high five. I gave him a slap.

"Truce?" he said, offering a sheepish grin.

I smiled back at him, and I almost meant it.

Gran and I went for dinner at Rocky's Roadhouse that evening. We sat at the bar so the three of us could hang out while Mom poured drinks. I couldn't stop yammering about my first day on the job. Mom and Gran beamed the entire time they listened to the details of my routine. Mom made sure to heap extra sweet-potato fries on my plate with the wings I ordered. She knew they were my favorite.

"Well, I hate to say I told you so, but didn't I say you'd like working, Dylan?" Gran said as she dipped a wing in honey-garlic sauce.

"And I hate to admit that you were right, Gran," I said, "but you were. Maybe for the first time ever."

When Gran shot me a killer glare, Mom stood there and laughed.

Chapter Eight

That night I remembered to set my alarm for six thirty. But on the morning of day two, I had too much time. Seven, I decided, would be the perfect time to get up.

I felt way more confident walking in on Wednesday morning. Before being told what to do, I started clearing tables, scraping food and loading the dishwasher.

Before long Hayden showed up, early like yesterday. I had a few questions to ask him and kept an eye out, waiting for my chance. I got it when I spotted him hauling a garbage bag out the back door. I hurried to catch up, pretending to have come to hold the door for him. He headed toward a row of giant garbage containers, and I followed.

"So, since you're the boss's son," I said, "it's okay to ask you questions, right? Since you're practically in charge here too?"

"Fire away," Hayden said, looking pleased.

"If I find the garbage can in the kitchen overflowing, is it okay for me to dispose of it out here? Then put a new bag in the can? I mean, I wouldn't want to be doing someone else's job."

"Of course," Hayden said. "My dad likes it when his employees take initiative."

"Cool," I said as we headed back to the kitchen. "So can I ask you one more thing? The T-shirt you had on the other day. Was it really a gift? Or did you maybe find it someplace?"

Uh-oh. Bad question, judging by how his face turned into a thunderhead.

"*Seriously*? Do you think I'm a Dumpster diver or something? You think I'd go digging around through trash for my clothes? Give me a break, Dylan." Hayden pushed past me and let the screen door slam in my face.

I might not be making friends with him anytime soon, but at least he'd answered my question. I hadn't said word one about digging through Dumpsters or trash. But he sure had. And now I had a fairly good idea where my clothes had wound up that night. So I could save Garrett's hide, if I wanted to.

Late that morning, I took a couple of calls at the desk. One of the callers wanted to adjust his dinner reservation to a later time on Friday night. I ran my finger down the list of names until I found his. I changed it from 8:00 PM to 9:00 PM. That was when I spotted the ink dot. Right beside the man's last name and phone number. It was barely noticeable.

The dot had *not* been there yesterday. I knew, because I had taken that call myself. Some guests gave cell phone numbers. Others had landlines at their cottages, and you could always tell by the first three numbers. This was a landline number.

Curious, I flipped back through the reservation book, studying each page closely. That was when I found a second dot. And a third. Lots of people press their pen tip onto the paper or doodle when they're on the phone. But on a hunch, I grabbed a notepad and scribbled down the phone numbers beside each dot.

Then I tore the paper off and crammed it into the pocket of my shorts.

"Dylan? What are you *doing*?" Tony, the line chef, stood behind me, frowning. "I need your help out in the kitchen."

"I was taking a phone call," I said.

"Clearly you *weren't*," Tony said, pointing to the phone sitting in its cradle. Then he came over and shut the reservation book. "This is confidential info, by the way. You shouldn't go flipping through this book, you know."

I felt my face start to burn. "But I just hung up," I said. "Someone called to change their dinner reservation."

"Whatever. Hurry up and get back here where we need you, okay?" he said.

As I scooted down the hall to the kitchen, I saw Mr. Hillier watching me through his open office door. The rest of the day, I busted my hump on the job. I even skipped my break.

Before I finished work that day, Mr. Hillier called me into his office. This time, his mouth was taut, with no trace of a smile.

"Maybe you can explain a couple of things to me," he said.

I gulped hard. "I'll try, sir," I told him.

"Why did you lie to Heather last Friday before I gave you the job?"

My face sizzled. What could I say? That Heather had covered for me by lying about why I was late? How had he even learned about that lie, anyway?

"Another question. Why were you snooping through the reservation book today?" His voice was harsh and accusing. I gulped again. "And *besides* that, you accused my son Hayden of digging through the trash today, too. What is your *problem*?"

"Um, Mr. Hillier—" I managed to choke out, then stopped. I couldn't even speak.

"Look, I don't tolerate dishonest employees," he said. I had a feeling I knew what was coming next. "You'd better not come back tomorrow, Dylan."

"Yes, sir," I said.

Then I spun around and walked out of his office. When I passed through the lobby, Heather was standing behind the reception desk, looking sad. Watching me get fired from my first job.

Riding my bike home that afternoon, I felt like throwing up. How could I explain this to Mom and Gran? They'd never forgive me, because they would totally believe what Mr. Hillier said. *Unless*...I braked my bike and dug into my pocket. The piece of paper was still there. Instead of heading for home, I parked in front of the

Bridgewood Weekly newspaper office on the main drag.

"Hey, Dylan." The photographer was sitting at his usual shabby desk when I walked in. He had photos up on a computer screen. "Long time no see."

I cringed. "That's probably a good thing," I said. I *so* hoped he wouldn't bring up the snowball incident from last winter.

"What's new?" The reporter smiled at me from behind her cluttered desk. "I'm sure you're not just dropping in to say hi."

"Nope," I said. Then I told them exactly what I needed. And they were more than happy to give it to me.

"You investigating something, Dylan?" the reporter asked. There was a glint of amusement in her eye. "You about to crack a case wide open or what?"

"Not sure," I said. "But if I do, I'm sure you'll be the first to know."

When I got home, Gran was making dinner. I hightailed it to my bedroom and pulled up the online phone directory. I knew that if you keyed in a phone number, it would show you that person's name and address. I tried the first number on the piece of paper from my pocket. Bingo. Then the second one. Bingo again.

I was right. The reporter had given me the names of the people who'd been robbed in the past couple of weeks. Those names corresponded with the ones that had an ink dot beside them in the reservation book. Both robberies had taken place while the cottagers were dining at Granitewood Lodge.

Now I was almost positive that the scheme had been set up at the reception desk. I had a pretty good idea I knew who it was too. Why else would Tony have freaked out about my looking through that reservation book?

All I had to do was prove it. That wasn't going to be easy. I had only one thing going for me. That last phone number, for the Friday-night dinner reservation I'd taken myself. The one that had an ink dot beside it in the reservation book this morning. It was the third phone number I'd jotted down. Now I had the address that went with the number. And that was going to save my skin.

I called Monica after dinner to tell her what had happened that day. She was nearly as shocked as I was. Then I begged for her help. I told her I needed somewhere to hide out all day. I wasn't ready to tell Mom and Gran what had happened. Not until I got it all sorted out. She offered her place, since her parents and two older brothers would be at work. She told me that if I got there around eight thirty on Thursday morning, everyone would be gone.

Monica was definitely the best thing about this summer so far.

Chapter Nine

All day Thursday, I chilled at Monica's place. I helped her weed her mom's garden. Then we played some video games and made sandwiches. It was smoking hot outside, but we couldn't risk going to the beach. If it got back to Mom somehow that I wasn't at work, questions would be asked, and I'd be doomed. So instead we sat under her sprinkler to cool off. We even shared a couple of kisses under there.

Later in the afternoon, I finally told Monica my version of the story. She was instantly caught up in the crazy plot, and she was willing to help me see my plan through to the end. Including staking out the robbery location after dark on Friday night. I told her I figured that Tony would make his move that night after his shift. That he would show up while the cottagers were dining at Granitewood, the way he had the last two times. Then he'd climb through a window and take their stuff.

"But you're going to tell Officer Vance for sure, right?" Monica said as I was about to head for home around four. "Because if Tony catches us there, who knows what he might do to us."

"Of course I'm telling her," I said as I climbed on my bike. "That's part of the plan. Imagine the look on Tony's face when Nicole and Prince show up. He'll be caught in the act. And *I'll* get my job back."

"Jeez, Dylan, I can't even believe all this is happening," Monica said, then shivered.

Which was a great opportunity to sneak in a hug before I rode off.

The two of us could barely sit still all day Friday. So far everything was going smoothly. Nobody suspected yet that I'd lost my job, and Monica's house was the perfect place to hang out. Before I left her place, we went over the plan carefully to make sure we both had it right.

"So you'll be out in front of the movie theater at eight," she said. "I already told my parents that we're going."

"Me too," I said. "It's all set. We'll head for the cottage and stake it out to watch Tony get caught. Our folks won't know how long the movie was. We'll be home before they even start to worry."

"Have you told Officer Vance yet?"

"That's where I'm going right now," I said. "To tell her what's happening tonight. So she can be there when it all goes down."

Nicole came out of a back office to greet me a few minutes after I asked for her at the desk.

"Dylan?" She frowned for a second. "How's the new job going?"

"Um, pretty good, I guess," I said as my face started to burn.

"Whew, that's a relief." Nicole gave me a crooked grin. "I was a bit worried. I ran into Tom Hillier in town on Wednesday afternoon. He mentioned how you showed up at the bonfire in the woods last week. And that you saved the day by calling nine-one-one. *Hah*!"

"*What*?" I clenched my fists. "And what did you *tell* him, Nicole?"

"Well, I laughed, of course, and told him he had his story wrong. And that you were just a bunch of innocent kids trying to have a good time."

I backed up and sank onto a bench against the wall. The one I'd been sitting on before making my statement to the cops on Saturday. "He fired me on Wednesday, Nicole. Because of what you told him," I said. "Among other things."

Nicole's eyes grew wide, and she sat down slowly beside me.

"Oh, Dylan. I didn't mean for that to happen. I'm so sorry. Did you tell your mom yet?"

"No, and don't bother telling her for me, okay? I'll tell her when I'm ready." I sighed.

"Look, I'll help you clear things up with your boss, okay?" she said. "We'll get this fixed, I promise."

"Actually, there's more to it," I said.

I told her everything else that had happened on Wednesday. And her eyes grew even wider.

"So it wasn't *entirely* my fault you lost your job, then. It was also about flipping through the reservation book. When you were *supposed* to be helping in the kitchen. And accusing the boss's son of digging through trash." Then Nicole's face split into a smile. "Wow, how do you manage to get yourself into so much trouble?"

I squinted at her. But I knew she was right. I had a habit of getting into hot water. And this time I wanted to get out of it, as fast as I could. And I knew she could help me.

"You owe me big-time," I said. "And here's what you need to do."

Then I told her exactly what I figured would be going on at the cottage that night. Her mouth fell open and stayed that way until I had finished.

"You mean to say that you know *when* and *where* the next robbery will be taking place? And you figured it out by snooping in the Granitewood reservation book and spotting some *ink dots*? Then googling some phone numbers? That sounds a bit far-fetched." Nicole rubbed her chin and stared into space.

"Just go to this address tonight. Like around ten, when it's dark, and wait and see what happens," I said. Then I handed her a piece of paper.

"I don't know, Dylan," she said, shaking her head. "I already have some suspects."

"But they're probably the wrong ones! *Please*, Nicole," I begged. "Consider it a Crime Stoppers tip, okay?"

"Okay." She shrugged. "Can't hurt, I guess." Then she narrowed her eyes. "But you *absolutely* cannot be there tonight."

Nuts. "I hear you," I said, then stood up and headed for the door.

Yup, I'd heard her loud and clear. But that didn't mean I would listen. Because there was no chance I was going to miss this.

I squirmed all through dinner that night. Gran stared at me across the table, her eyebrows dancing a jig. She asked me if I had ants in my pants. I told her I was excited about my movie date with Monica. She gave me a sweet, grand-motherly smile.

Monica was waiting for me outside the movie theater, as planned. We didn't have much choice at the run-down Bridgewood movie theater. There were only ever two films playing, and one was always an animated family flick. We chose the other one, which was a scary movie. Good choice for the cuddle factor. Every time the villain snuck up on the victim, Monica crammed herself even closer to me.

The show let out close to ten. We couldn't possibly have timed it better. The sky had grown inky black. Instead of heading for home, the two of us, holding hands, headed in the direction of the cottage road on the edge of town. It was only a few blocks away, like everything in Bridgewood. I could feel Monica shivering beside me, and I put my arm around her and squeezed her shoulder.

"Quit worrying," I said. "Nothing is going to happen."

"I can't help it. I'm still nervous," she said.

The bush closed in around us when we reached the cottage road. I already knew the address by heart. It was just a matter of finding it in the dark. Too bad we were both dumb enough to forget to bring flashlights. We stumbled along, glad for the light from neighboring cottages. That light was how I managed to pick out the target cottage. We sidled along the edge of the road, searching for a good place to hide. The cottage owners had left only one light on. I hooked my arm through Monica's and led her through the trees and shrubs that surrounded the cottage.

"Stick with me. I think we can get in pretty close," I said.

In a few seconds, we were close enough that we'd be able to hear anyone coming along the laneway. Maybe even see him in the dim light. And, from our hiding spot, we'd be sure to have a good view of Nicole's takedown. We crouched there and waited for something to happen.

A few minutes later, something *did* happen.

Chapter Ten

A heavy hand landed on my shoulder. On Monica's too, judging by her yelp.

"Okay, you two, let's go."

We both spun around. A flashlight flicked on, practically blinding me. But I could tell who was holding it. A police officer was standing there, and he did not look thrilled.

"What the heck?" I said. "What's going on?"

"I was hoping you could tell me that," the officer said. "And I'm sure you will once we're in the cruiser."

"But what...where did you even come from?" I asked. I groped for Monica's hand and clutched it tightly. Her hand was clammy and shaking. Mine was too.

"I was standing behind this tree." He patted the thick trunk of a pine. "We got a tip about this. And here you are, right on schedule. You kids need to find better things to do with your time than ripping off cottagers."

"What?" I almost shouted. "Where's Nicole Vance tonight, anyway?"

"Just happening to know an officer's name won't get you off the hook, you know." He took us both by the arm. "Let's get moving."

"But I'm the one who gave Nicole the tip! Where is she?"

"Officer Vance finished her shift at five." The officer's voice was gruff and no-nonsense. "Come on. Let's get you kids home to your parents, and we'll take it from there."

When I looked at Monica, big fat tears were rolling down her cheeks.

"We are *so* doomed," she said.

The officer lit the laneway with his flashlight. We followed the beam to his cruiser, which was parked a ways down the cottage road. It was backed up against a hedge. And unmarked too. We'd waltzed right past it without a clue. I felt like the biggest dope on the planet.

Monica and I sat in the back seat, vibrating with dread. The officer sat in the front seat, looking at a computer screen. That was when we heard footsteps crunching on the gravel road.

As they neared the car, I nudged Monica with my elbow.

"Uh, officer," I got up the nerve to say. "This might be the person that you actually *should* be looking for. I mean, instead of us."

The officer shifted in his seat and turned his head sideways. "When I need your advice, I'll ask for it," he said. "Give me a minute here and…"

Then he stopped talking and held up one hand. In the dim light from a nearby cottage, we could make out the shape of someone approaching who clearly wasn't out for a stroll. This person was skulking along and seemed to be trying to avoid the light.

"Okay, you two, don't move a muscle," the officer said to us. Then he quietly climbed out of the car and crept off into the darkness.

I wouldn't have been able to move even if I'd wanted to. Monica's hand was clamped on my arm, and she wouldn't let go.

"Don't you dare even *think* of trying to follow him," she hissed. "We're already in enough trouble."

"Can't anyway," I said. "Cruiser door's locked."

"Why did I even listen to your dumb plan, Dylan?" Monica said.

Then I heard her gulp back a sob. Maybe it was a dumb plan after all. Maybe if I'd listened to Nicole this afternoon, we wouldn't be sitting in the back of a cruiser. But I sure didn't want to admit that to Monica.

A few minutes later we heard voices. The officer was leading someone toward the car. Then he yanked open the door.

"Squeeze over, you two," he said.

"What the heck…" I said as Heather slid into the back seat, her face blotchy and wet.

"Dylan!" She turned and hugged me. "Thank goodness you're here. Maybe you can explain things to this cop!"

Beside me, Monica leaned forward for a better look.

"Oh, Heather the hugger." Then she pinched my arm so hard that I yelped. "Hah. Real good detective work, Dylan," Monica said with a snort.

"What are you doing out here in the dark anyway, Heather?" I said.

"Well obviously, trying to track down the jewelry thieves," Heather said. "But this policeman won't listen to what I'm telling him."

"Oh." That was all I could say before my mouth went dry. Something Heather had said was making me shrivel up inside. Jewelry thieves? Nicole wouldn't tell me what had been stolen during the last robbery. *Might compromise the investigation*, she'd said.

So how did Heather know that jewelry had been stolen?

"Honestly, officer, you have to listen to me. I know who was behind those robberies. I know exactly how it happened too. And I'll tell you right now."

Heather's voice was white noise droning in my ear. I wished I was home in bed instead of sitting in the backseat of a squad car. She was yammering on about Tony and how she'd come here tonight to catch him in the act. She said she'd suspected him all along. I couldn't believe what was coming out of her mouth. Then the officer cut her off mid-sentence.

"There's only one problem with your story, young lady."

"Huh?" Heather said through a couple of loud snuffles.

"It wasn't public knowledge that jewelry was stolen. How did you know that?"

Silence. Heather started to cry even louder, this time for real. Monica leaned in closer and put her head on my shoulder.

"Sorry I pinched you, Dylan," she said. "And one more thing. *Never* trust a super hugger."

The police officer dropped Monica and me off at home. Which was a total relief. I was safe in bed by eleven. Gran and Mom didn't need to know what had happened that night—at least, not yet. Lying there under my covers, relief settled over me. Now that Heather was a robbery suspect, Garrett and his friends would be off the hook. I figured the two of us would be on better terms from here on in. Maybe my friends would be off the hook now too. And their parents would set them free for the summer.

I was pretty sure Heather would be unemployed. I planned to be at Granitewood Lodge bright and early the next morning. It was time to explain a few things to my ex-boss, Mr. Hillier.

When I walked through the door just before nine on Saturday, his eyebrows shot up.

"What are you doing here, Dylan?" he said.

"I need to explain some stuff, Mr. Hillier," I said. "I hope you're willing to listen."

Mr. Hillier leaned against the check-in desk. He raised one eyebrow at me.

"This better be worth my time," he said. "Start talking."

It was cool to see the changes his face went through while I told my story. His mouth opened and closed like a trout's. His dark eyebrows bobbed. He shook his head in disbelief.

"You mean to say that you had all this figured out from looking through that reservation book? And that this time you *did* tip off the police?"

Burning face again. "Heather lied for me that day," I said. "I told her the truth about why I was late for my job interview. And she's the one who changed my story. Then on Wednesday, Officer Vance told you what really happened."

"And then I fired you for lying." He pursed his lips. "So I think I owe you an apology. And a job. Maybe you'd like to work the reservation desk. I'm sure we'll be needing someone."

Something like fireworks went off in my head. "Seriously? That would be awesome!"

"Excellent," Mr. Hillier said. "But I need you to answer one question first."

"What's that, sir?" I said.

He frowned. "Why did you accuse Hayden of garbage picking the other day?"

"Well, I didn't actually accuse him. I asked him where he got his T-shirt. That's all." I tried to smile. I wanted to put that nasty towel incident behind me forever.

"Yeah, he's right, Dad." Hayden had stepped into the lobby. He offered me a shaky smile. "And I accused Dylan of accusing me of garbage picking. But I actually did find a cool skateboard T-shirt in the garbage bin on Saturday morning, along with some other stuff. I took out the T-shirt and buried the rest under the trash."

"Why were you even in the garbage bin though?" I said.

Mr. Hillier smirked. "We like to check it every morning to make sure other people aren't dumping stuff in our trash containers. Unfortunately, that's Hayden's job."

"So I guess I am a Dumpster diver," Hayden said, then laughed. "Sorry I gave you a hard time that day. Thought it would look bad to admit the boss's son went shopping in a garbage bin. So I told my dad what you said to me. I didn't mean to help you get fired though."

I shrugged. "Can I just have my T-shirt back?" I asked him.

They both stared at me. "Wait, it's *your* T-shirt?" Hayden said.

And I had to tell that towel story all over again. Then try to smile while they laughed their heads off. Well, at least I had a job again.

Only this time, it was an even better one.

Deb Loughead is the author of more than twenty-five books for children and young adults ranging from poetry and plays to picture books and novels, many in translation. Her award-winning poetry and prose have appeared in a variety of Canadian publications. Deb likes to spend her non-writing time reading, knitting, walking her dog Cleo, or hanging out close to the water in cottage country. She lives with her family in Toronto, Ontario.

orca *currents*

For more information on all the books
in the Orca Currents series, please visit
www.orcabook.com